TAP
TAP
BOOM
BOOM

For Jake,
who brings sunshine
and friendship
to any rainy day

E. B.

For Zachary,
braver of storms

G. B. K.

TAP TAP BOOM BOOM

Elizabeth Bluemle — illustrated by G. Brian Karas

CANDLEWICK PRESS

Tap **TAP,**

dark clouds.

Tap **TAP,**

damp air.

Tap **TAP,**

cold drops
of rain
dot hair.

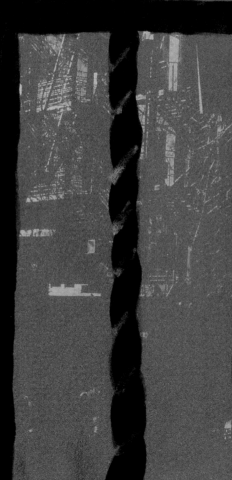
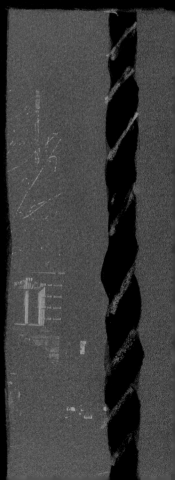

Street carts appear:
"Umbrellas here!"

Tap **TAP**

Tap **TAP**

BOOM

BOOM

Tap **TAP**
Tap **TAP**
BOOM
BOOM
Crackle-
BOOM

Got a storm,
big storm
in bloom,
here soon.

Sky grumbles.
Rain tumbles.
Big weather—
you'd better . . .

get under
umbrella!

BOOM

BOOM

That's right—
slam bang!
Hold tight
to umbrella.
Wind whirls
helter-skelter.

BOOM
BOOM

Tap **TAP,**
tap **TAP.**
Slap feet,
shoes flap.
Feet wetter?
You'd better
go down
underground,
where the water
can't getcha.
You betcha.

Now harder!
Now faster!

Big rain
side blaster.

The subway
is shelter.

BOOM
BOOM

Downstairs
we wait.
Folks
congregate.

We squeeze.

Whose feet
and knees
are these?

Hey, hey!
Watch spray!
We get
more wet.

Tap **TAP**
Tap **TAP**
BOOM
BOOM

See
big, big fellow
with tiny
umbrella.
It's yellow.

Tap **TAP**
BOOM
BOOM

One girl
all fancy.
She's late
for dancing.

Can't wait!
Fast dash
after
lightning flash.

The storm
above
makes friends
of strangers.

We laugh
under cover
at thunder
and danger.

Tall lady
   with poodle
      sees kid—no umbrella.

Hands hers.
   No words,
      just a smile
         as her hello.

Two friends descend,
huddled close
from weather.

Wet sides.
Smiles wide.
Together
is better.

Storm
ending soon.
No tap.
No boom.
Outside
clear light.
Bright afternoon.

We race
upstairs.
Shake drops
off hair.

"Look up!"
we cry.

Surprise in sky.

Now people
scatter

through puddle
splatter.

We wave
good-bye.

"So long!"
"Keep dry!"

'Til the next
Tap **TAP**
Tap **TAP**
BOOM
BOOM

'Til the next

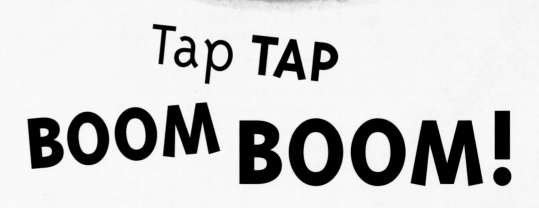

Tap **TAP**
BOOM BOOM!